ADAM'S ANIMALS

By Barry L. Schwartz

Illustrated by Steliyana Doneva

This **PJ BOOK** belongs to

_____

_____

PJ Library®

JEWISH BEDTIME STORIES and SONGS

APPLES & HONEY PRESS

Springfield, NJ • Jerusalem

And God formed out of the earth all the wild beasts and birds of the sky, and brought them to the man to see what he would call them; and whatever the man called each living creature, that would be its name.

Genesis 2:19

Dedicated to the children of
Congregation Adas Emuno, Leonia, New Jersey
—BLS

To children everywhere,
who see the world through pure eyes
—SD

A note from the author:
This book is a *midrash*; following in the time-honored tradition of commentary that "fills in the gaps" of Torah. We elaborate on how Adam named all the creatures (Genesis 2:19-20). We show Adam waking up to Eve's presence, because we are taught that Adam was created first and Eve was "fashioned from the rib" of Adam (Genesis 2:22). In another account, the Torah tells us that they were created simultaneously, "male and female God created them" (Genesis 1:27), and so we depict Eve fully formed, with her name already in place.

Apples & Honey Press
An imprint of Behrman House and Gefen Publishing House
Behrman House, 11 Edison Place, Springfield, New Jersey 07081
Gefen Publishing House Ltd., 6 Hatzvi Street, Jerusalem 94386, Israel
www.applesandhoneypress.com

Text copyright © 2017 by Barry L. Schwartz
Illustrations copyright © 2017 by Apples & Honey Press

ISBN 978-1-68115-530-2

Library of Congress Cataloging-in-Publication Data

Names: Schwartz, Barry L., author. | Doneva, Steliyana, illustrator.
Title: Adam's animals / by Barry L. Schwartz ; illustrated by Steliyana Doneva.
Description: Springfield, NJ : Apples & Honey Press, [2017] | Summary: "In the beginning…. Adam said to the animals, 'I need to name you.' Adam gives a name to every animal, from the aardvark and the aardwolf to the bandicoot and the bongo, all the way to the zebra and the zebu"-- Provided by publisher.
Identifiers: LCCN 2016045324 | ISBN 9781681155302
Subjects: | CYAC: Animals--Fiction. | Adam (Biblical figure)--Fiction. | Alphabet.
Classification: LCC PZ7.1.S33657 Ad 2017 | DDC [E]--dc23 LC record available at https://lccn.loc.gov/2016045324

Designed by Alexandra N. Segal
Edited by Dena Neusner
Printed in China

1 3 5 7 9 8 6 4 2
101725.3K1/B1098/A4

In the beginning, after the darkness,

the world was full of light.

The earth was covered by deep blue seas and pale blue skies.

Sometimes the puffy white clouds turned dark and rainy.

Mountains started multiplying, rivers started running . . .

and dry land appeared.

Seeds started sprouting, bushes started budding . . .

and delicious fruits appeared.

The sun shone by day;
the moon and stars by night.
Fish started swimming, birds started flying,
and animals were everywhere.

A tall, two-legged creature appeared. . . .

Meet Adam.

Adam smiled when he was happy and cried when he was sad.

Adam laughed when
he was pleased
and frowned when
he was puzzled.

Sometimes Adam was
a hard worker,
and sometimes he rested.

Most of all, Adam liked
to walk with the animals
and talk to the animals.

One day Adam said to them,

"I need to name you."

All the animals crowded around Adam to receive their names.

First came the lions and tigers and bears.

(Oh my!)

Then the giraffes, who kept bumping their heads.

The elephants squeezed their way to the front of the crowd.

The ants almost got squished.

"Stop!" said Adam.

"Everyone form a single line."

The line was very, very, VERY long.

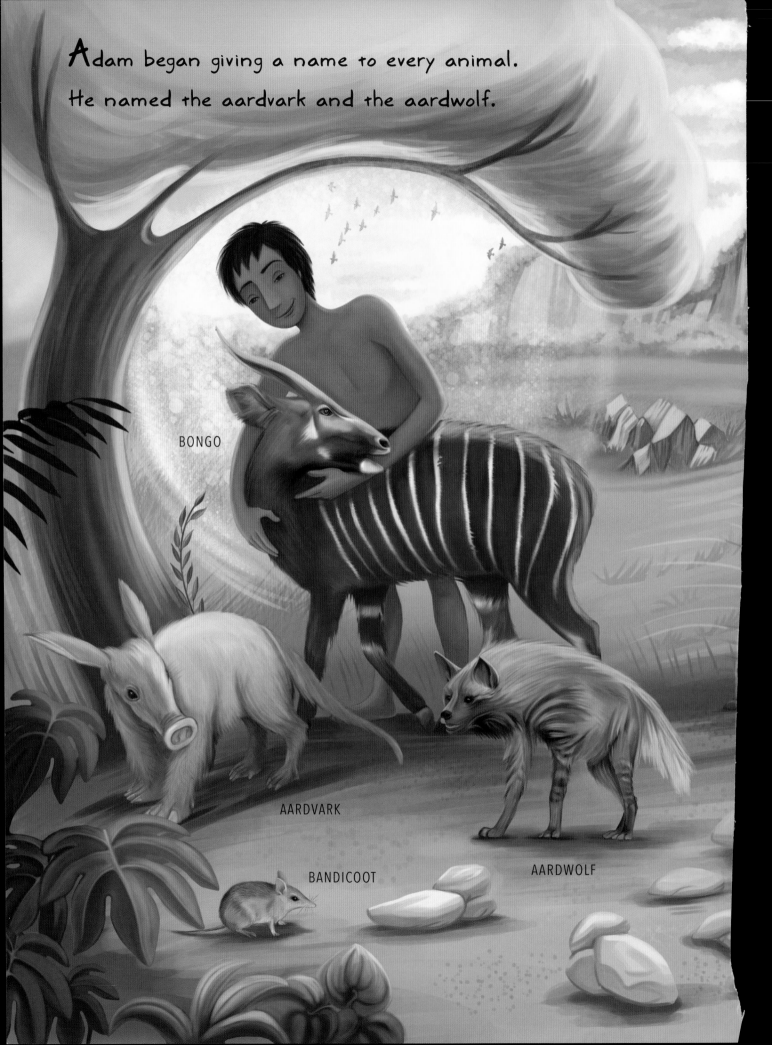

Adam began giving a name to every animal.
He named the aardvark and the aardwolf.

BONGO

AARDVARK

BANDICOOT

AARDWOLF

He named the bandicoot and the bongo,

the caiman and the caracal,

the dabchick and the dik-dik.

CARACAL

DIK-DIK

DABCHICK

CAIMAN

Adam named the egret and the emu,
the ferret and the firebrat,
the gecko and the grebe.

KINKAJOU

HOOPOE

LEMUR

IBEX

JAGUAR

KING COBRA

FIREBRAT

He named the hippo and the hoopoe,
the ibex and the ibis,
the jackal and the jaguar.

MATAMATA

He named the king cobra and the kinkajou,
the lemming and the lemur,
the matamata and the meerkat.

And still the animals kept coming.

UINTA SQUIRREL

RHEA

URIAL

TOPI

QUAIL

NEWT

TAPIR

VIPER

Adam named the narwhal and the newt,
the ocelot and the octopus,
the pollock and the pudu.

NARWHAL

He named the quail and the quoll,
the rhea and the rhesus,
the skink and the skunk.

VULTURE

PUDU

RHESUS

OCELOT

QUOLL

SKUNK

SKINK

He named the tapir and the topi,
the uinta squirrel and the urial,
the viper and the vulture.

OCTOPUS

POLLOCK

Adam named the wallaby and the warthog,

the xenops and the xerus,
the yak and the yapok.

YAK

ZEBU

WARTHOG

WALLABY

YAPOK

XERUS

And let's not forget the zebra and the zebu!

ZEBRA

XENOPS

Now most of the animals were pleased
with their names.
But some were not.
The yellow-bellied sapsucker wished
Adam had paid attention to
her pretty red head instead.

YELLOW-BELLIED
SAPSUCKER

PINK FAIRY ARMADILLO

The blue-footed booby positively preferred turquoise.
The pink fairy armadillo sought something rosier.

BLUE-FOOTED BOOBY

Once these animals complained, others started to come forward.

STINKBUG

BLOBFISH

The stinkbug thought her name was smelly.

The blobfish thought his name was messy.

The pufferfish thought her name was puffy.

PUFFERFISH

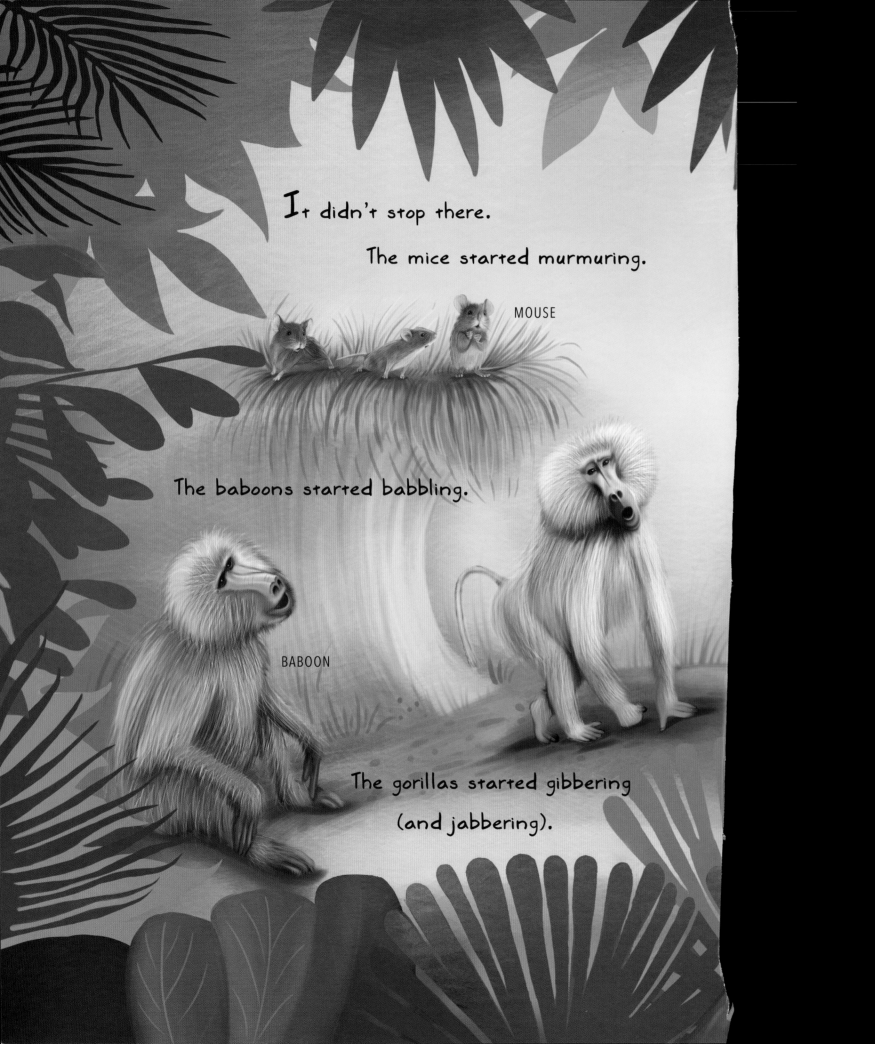

It didn't stop there.

The mice started murmuring.

MOUSE

The baboons started babbling.

BABOON

The gorillas started gibbering
(and jabbering).

GORILLA

Adam said, "You'll just have to do the best you can with the name you are given."

When Adam was finally finished naming
every last critter, and finally finished
cleaning up all of the you-know-what,
he looked around.

The garden was green but silent,
clean but empty, bright but dreary.
All the animals had gone home.
Adam was lonely.

Adam fell asleep, alone. When he awoke there was someone beside him, someone who looked a lot like him . . . only a bit different.

For once, Adam was at a loss for words.

Finally he said, "Should I name you?"

"I already have a name," said the someone.

"It's Eve."

"What a lovely name," Adam said. "Would you be my partner?"
Eve smiled. "That would be nice."

"Let's go for a walk," said Adam. "I have a few friends
for you to meet."

Off they went, hand in hand.

Barry L. Schwartz

is director of The Jewish Publication Society in Philadelphia
and rabbi of Congregation Adas Emuno in Leonia, New Jersey.
He is the author of *Judaism's Great Debates; Jewish Heroes,
Jewish Values; Jewish Theology: A Comparative Study;* and
Honi the Circlemaker: Eco-Fables from Ancient Israel.

Steliyana Doneva

began her career as an animator in a movie animation studio.
She has an MA in Graphic Arts from St. Cyril and St. Methodius
University of Veliko Turnovo in Bulgaria. In addition to illustrating
children's books, she enjoys photography and making fabric toys.
She lives in Sofia, Bulgaria.